Fresh Fish

John Kilaka

Fresh Fish

A Groundwood Book   Douglas & McIntyre   Toronto   Vancouver   Berkeley

weg.

Sokwe Chimpanzee was rowing home with a boat full of fish. He dreamed about how much money he would make selling his catch at the market the next day.

But as he drew near the shore, he began to hear music. His friends were having a party.

The music was irresistible. Sokwe just had to join in and dance. The boat almost tipped over as he dropped his oar into the lake.

He stopped dancing long enough to gather up the fish and attach them to a pole. Then he set off toward his house.

I'll just leave these at home, he thought, and then come back to the party.

On the way, Sokwe ran into his friends Dog, Zebra and Leopard. They had their drums and were hurrying off to play with the others.

When Dog saw the fish, he stopped dead in his tracks.

"Oh, Sokwe, what a wonderful catch!" he said. "But you are carrying far too much. Let me help you with that nice big fat one. After all, what are friends for?" His voice was sugary. "Don't worry, I'll give it back as soon as we get to your house."

Sokwe knew perfectly well what was going on.

"Thanks anyway," he said. "But just take this fat one and keep it. I'm sure you'll enjoy it."

Sokwe and his friends set off to market early the next morning. Dog, Zebra, Mrs. Hippopotamus, Pig, Leopard, Mrs. Monkey and Lion hitched a ride in the back of the truck, and Mrs. Hare sat in front. All but Dog were laden with things to sell.

"Are you only coming along to buy?" Sokwe asked curiously, as he noticed Dog edging closer and closer to the baskets of fish.

On the way, they saw cats and mice having a party of their own. Sokwe stopped the truck so that everyone could watch. Dog took advantage of the situation and stuck his paws into the fish basket, but clever Mrs. Hare had been keeping an eye on him.

"Shame on you," she called out. "Stealing from your friend."

"Is this how you thank me for giving you a fish yesterday?" grumbled Sokwe. "Don't do it again."

Dog mumbled and promised to be good.

Suddenly everyone heard a loud bang.

"Oh, no! A flat tire! Now we're really going to be late to market," exclaimed all the animals.

"Don't worry," Mrs. Hare said. "I can fix it. I just need a jack to lift the truck."

"No problem," answered Lion. "Unload everything and I will hold it up."

So everyone pitched in and in no time the tire was removed, patched, filled with air and replaced.

Instead of helping, Dog was soon caught sniffing around the baskets again. Mrs. Monkey shook her finger at him and warned him to watch himself.

But no one was paying attention when he snuck behind the truck with a sharp nail he had found on the ground.

Very soon they were at the market. Bananas, melons and oranges were piled high. Sokwe immediately set up his table and began to play his mbira to attract customers. The other animals were so busy buying and selling that almost no one noticed when Dog snuck up to the fish basket and helped himself.

Suddenly a loud roar filled the market.

"Stop, thief!" bellowed Lion. But as he ran to catch Dog, he slid into Mrs. Monkey and tripped over Mrs. Hippopotamus's basket of oranges.

"OW, my leg!" he cried.

The animals bustled around poor Lion, who was moaning on the ground. No one saw Dog run off into the mountains with his prize.

"It's a good thing we've got the truck," said Sokwe. "You need to get to the hospital."

Mrs. Monkey cut down some branches, and helpful Mrs. Hare explained how to make a stretcher.

All the animals were needed to carry Lion to the truck, but when they arrived, they found two flat tires. A rusty nail was sticking out of one of them. Mrs. Monkey remembered that she had seen Dog carrying a nail just like it when she'd caught him sniffing around the fish before.

"And I saw him fooling around the tires," said Lion miserably.

It was a long way to the hospital, and many of the animals were cursing Dog by the time they staggered in under Lion's weight.

Luckily it was a very modern place. Mrs. Hippopotamus even decided to have her teeth fixed while she was there.

Bone doctor Frog examined Lion's leg. "Broken, I see," he croaked. "I'm afraid this will have to come off."

The animals shrieked. How would they ever carry a three-legged animal all the way home?

"Just a moment, Doctor," wise Mrs. Hare said. "Take it easy. Why not just put his leg in a cast?"

Dr. Frog hemmed and hawed. "All right, I'll try."

After giving Lion an injection, he wrapped his leg so it wouldn't bend. A crutch completed the cure. The animals thanked Dr. Frog and set off on the long trip home.

JOHN KILAKA

The next morning, after a good sleep, the animals gathered for the Junior Soccer Championship. Everyone was there except Dog. There was a lot of talk about what he had done and where he might be.

The game began. Sokwe was the referee. He had made himself a special whistle.

The young lions stormed down the field and scored almost immediately. Then the other young animals came back with a goal of their own. The lions responded with a fierce advance. But while their strength was an advantage, they lacked experience.

They were taken by surprise by the weaker animals. Young Hare caught a pass and forwarded it to young Tortoise. Young Sokwe received it next and gave a mighty kick. The lions' goalkeeper ducked as the ball flew past him and hit Mrs. Hippopotamus right smack on her new teeth, then bounced off and broke a goal post.

The game came to a temporary halt while Sokwe and some of the other parents went off to look for a new goal post. As they were walking along, their eyes caught a flash of red. When they ran over to investigate, they found the fish thief himself, sleeping off his feast in the hollow trunk of a baobab tree, surrounded by evidence of his crime!

They woke him up and tied his paws together before taking him back to the village. The animals were very shocked and decided to build a prison for Dog at once. Even though the young lions complained bitterly, the soccer game was over.

A few days later, there was a trial.

Elephant, as village elder, read out the very serious charges. First, Dog had punctured the back tires of the truck. Second, he had stolen and eaten his friend Sokwe's fish. Third, because of Dog's actions, Lion had broken his leg.

Dog immediately pled guilty to everything. So Elephant pronounced the sentence.

"The accused is guilty of all three charges. Now he must work extra hard for the village on Tree Planting Day. He and his family will have to plant twice as many trees as the rest of us."

Even though Lion who was in charge of overseeing the sentence had staked out an enormous field, Dog and his family worked so hard and so fast that they were finished before the others.

When the trees had all been planted, some animals went back to the market to fix the truck and bring it home. Meanwhile, those who stayed behind cooked a huge feast, and that evening there was much joyous eating and celebrating.

Sokwe danced with his old friend Dog. All was forgiven. And when the party drew to a close, hands were shaken all around.

"Sleep well. See you tomorrow," the animals called out to each other as they headed home to their peaceful beds.

Copyright © 2001 by Atlantis, an imprint of Orell Füssli Verlag AG, Zürich, Switzerland
All rights reserved
English text copyright © 2005 by Groundwood Books
First published in English in 2005 by Groundwood Books by arrangement with Baobab

Groundwood Books / Douglas & McIntyre
720 Bathurst Street, Suite 500, Toronto, Ontario
Distributed in the USA by Publishers Group West
1700 Fourth Street, Berkeley, CA 94710

Library and Archives Canada Cataloguing in Publication
Kilaka, John
Fresh fish / John Kilaka.
Translation of: Frische fische.
ISBN 0-88899-656-X
I. Title.
PZ7.K54Fr 2005   j823'.92   C2004-905064-8

Printed and bound in China